A Note to Parents

For many children, learning math math!" is their first response — to wl add "Me, too!" Children often see a and writing, but they rarely have such models for mathematics. And math fear can be catching!

The easy-to-read stories in this **Hello Math Reader!** series were written to give children a positive introduction to mathematics and parents a pleasurable re-acquaintance with a subject that is important to everyone's life. **Hello Math Reader!** stories make mathematical ideas accessible, interesting, and fun for children. The activities and suggestions at the end of each book provide parents with a hands-on approach to help children develop mathematical interest and confidence.

Enjoy the mathematics!
• Give your child a chance to retell the story. The more familiar children are with the story, the more they will understand its mathematical concepts.
• Use the colorful illustrations to help children "hear and see" the math at work in the story.
• Treat the math activities as games to be played for fun. Follow your child's lead. Spend time on those activities that engage your child's interest and curiosity.
• Activities, especially ones using physical materials, help make abstract mathematical ideas concrete.

Learning is a messy process and learning about math calls for children to become immersed in lively experiences that help them make sense of mathematical concepts and symbols.

Although learning about numbers is basic to math, other ideas, such as identifying shapes and patterns, measuring, collecting and interpreting data, reasoning logically, and thinking about chance are also important. By reading these stories and having fun with the activities, you will help your child enthusiastically say "**Hello, math**," instead of "I hate math."

—Marilyn Burns
National Mathematics Educator
Author of *The I Hate Mathematics! Book*

For Kathryn Bennett
— S.K.

For Mom and Dad
— L.C.

ISBN 0-439-30472-5

Library of Congress Cataloging-in-Publication Data

Keenan, Sheila.
    The trouble with pets / by Sheila Keenan ; illustrated by Laura Coyle;
    math activities by Marilyn Burns.
       p.   cm.— (Hello reader! Math. Level 3)
    "Cartwheel books"
    Summary: Myrtle's pet shop specializes in animals that swim, until the day
that several strange boxes are left on her doorstep. Includes related multiplication
activities.
    ISBN 0-439-30472-5
    [1. Pets—Fiction. 2. Multiplication—Fiction. 3. Arithmetic—fiction.]
  I. Coyle, Laura, ill. II. Burns, Marilyn. III. title. IV. Series.
  PZ7.3.K2295 My 2001
  [E] — dc21   2001020435

10 9 8 7 6 5 4 3 2 1   01 02 03 04 05

Printed in the U.S.A.   24
First printing, November 2001

The Trouble with Pets

with

Pets

by Sheila Keenan
Illustrated by Laura Coyle
Math Activities by Marilyn Burns

Hello Math Reader! — Level 3

SCHOLASTIC INC.
New York   Toronto   London   Auckland   Sydney
Mexico City   New Delhi   Hong Kong

At the corner of Water Street
was a building you couldn't miss.
It was bright blue with green trim.
It had two floors,
five windows,
and a door shaped like a porthole.

The first floor was a pet shop called
Myrtle's Turtles.
Myrtle herself lived on the second floor.
(Although she didn't keep any pets.)

You could always get turtles
at Myrtle's Turtles.
You could get fish, frogs, and salamanders
there, too.
On a good day, she might even have an eel.
"I like things that swim," said Myrtle.

Early one morning,
Myrtle was curled up all warm and cozy
in her water bed.

RINNNNGG! RINNNNGG! RINNNNGG!
Someone rang her doorbell —
over and over and over.

Myrtle rolled out of bed.
She threw open the window
and saw a brown truck drive off.
She saw something else, too.

Myrtle ran downstairs,
unlocked the door,
and peeked out.

There was a wooden box on her doorstep.
It had slats across the top.
It had holes along the sides.
It had 20 little noses poking out of it.

Myrtle picked up the box
and looked inside.
Forty beady little eyes looked back.
"Mice!" cried Myrtle.

Myrtle brought the box into her shop.
"I must return this," she said.
She turned the box around, looking for a label.

The latch slid open.
Twenty little white mice scurried out.

Five of them headed straight for
a big bag of fish flakes.
Five of them swarmed the turtle pen.
Five of them slid into the frog pond.
And five mice just disappeared from sight.

Myrtle was so busy chasing the mice,
that she didn't hear the doorbell.

Someone called out, "Anybody home?"

"I'm coming," Myrtle said.
But she didn't get there fast enough.

There was already a cardboard box on her doorstep. It had holes all around it and a screen top.

"Do I hear purring?" asked Myrtle.

Myrtle carried the box into her shop.
Ten furry little tails hung out of its holes.

She set the box down and peered
through the screen top.

"Kittens!" said Myrtle.
"Kittens don't like to swim.
This is not the pet store for them.
I must return this box, too."

Myrtle knelt down on one side
of the box to look for a label.
On the other side, the kittens scratched away
at a hole.
When the hole was big enough,
they squeezed out, one by one.

Ten little kitten noses sniffed around:
Mice!
The kittens were off!

Two chased mice over the eel.

Two chased mice under the salamanders.

Two chased mice along the shelves.

Two chased mice behind the counter.

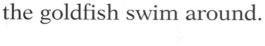

And two kittens just stopped to watch
the goldfish swim around.

"Delivery!" somebody called.
"Oh, no," said Myrtle.

Myrtle was careful not to step
on any of the tails and paws
that kept getting underfoot.

By the time she got to the door,
nobody was there.
But there was a big crate on the
sidewalk.

Myrtle moved closer to the crate
and looked through its holes.

Twenty-four eyes stared back.

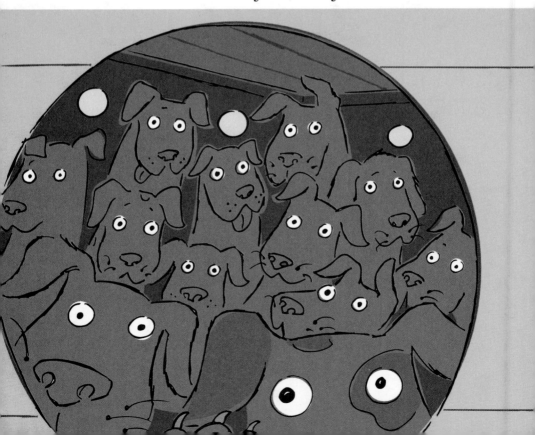

She walked around the crate
to the other side.
Twelve tails started thumping.
There were a few yips, too.

"Hmm," Myrtle said. She slowly
lifted the top of the crate.
"Sounds like, smells like, looks like
PUPPIES!" she cried.

A dozen little dogs jumped
out of the crate.
They raced into Myrtle's pet shop.
Myrtle raced in after them.

"Down," she said. "Sit! Stay! Heel!
STOP!"

One little puppy did sit down,
right on Myrtle's shoe.

But the other 11 puppies
went right after the kittens.

Myrtle's Turtles was a big mess!
Puppies leaped in and out of the tanks.
Kittens swished their paws in the fish bowls.
Mice ate anything they could find —
and tried not to get eaten themselves!

Myrtle decided to save the mice first.
She began to scoop them up in pairs.
"2, 4, 6, 8, 10 . . . " she counted.

Then the doorbell rang again.
Myrtle froze in her tracks.

"Excuse me," a voice said.
"I was expecting some boxes.
Were they left here?"

Pavi, Myrtle's new neighbor, walked in.
She looked at the mess. "I'm so sorry," she said.
"But I have an idea."

Pavi came back with a box of dog treats and
a bag of catnip.
She shook the box and waved the bag around.
Then she slowly backed out of the store.

The kittens and puppies fell into line
right behind her.

All except one little puppy . . .

who hid behind Myrtle.
Myrtle looked down at the puppy.
The puppy looked up at Myrtle.
He licked her face.

Pavi came back to help clean up.
"Is that a real eel?" she asked.
"Would you like to swap for it?"
Myrtle answered.
"Because I like things that swim . . .
but I like puppy kisses, too!"

• ABOUT THE ACTIVITIES •

Learning about multiplication is one of the major goals of elementary school mathematics. It's beneficial to prepare young children before they formally study this important concept by giving them experience with counting equal groups—the foundation to understanding multiplication. This foundation is best built by engaging children in activities that give them opportunities to think about equal groups in real-world contexts. Counting by twos, fours, fives, and other numbers also helps develop children's number sense, an important part of arithmetic understanding. Figuring out the number of feet on ten mice or the number of eyes on a dozen puppies are examples of the skill building you'll find in *The Trouble with Pets* and the activities that follow.

While the correct notation for multiplication is introduced in these activities, learning this notation or memorizing multiplication tables is not the goal for young children. The focus for introducing multiplication should be on helping children see when and why multiplication is useful, how it relates to real-world situations, and how it connects to other arithmetic operations, specifically addition and division.

Enjoy the story and the activities with your child!
—Marilyn Burns

You'll find tips and suggestions for guiding the activities whenever you see a box like this!

Retelling the Story

In the wooden box delivered to Myrtle's doorstep, Myrtle saw 20 noses poking out. What animals were they?

The 20 little white mice scurried out of the box in four groups of five. Where did each group go? Count by fives to check that four fives make 20: 5, 10, 15, 20.

Ten furry little tails hung out of the cardboard box delivered to Myrtle's doorstep. What animals were they?

The ten little kittens set off in five groups of two. Where did each group go? Count by twos to check that five twos make 10: 2, 4, 6, 8, 10.

When Myrtle looked in the crate delivered to the sidewalk, she saw 24 eyes. Then 12 tails started thumping. What animals were they?

Count by twos to check that 12 puppies have 24 eyes: 2, 4, 6, 8, 10, 12, 14, 16, 18, 20, 22, 24. What happened when the puppies jumped out of the crate?

Myrtle scooped up the mice in pairs: 2, 4, 6, 8, 10, 12, 14, 16, 18, 20. How many pairs do 20 mice make?

Myrtle's new neighbor, Pavi, rang the doorbell. What happened next?

The kittens followed Pavi in rows of five: 5, 10. Two fives make 10. The puppies followed Pavi in rows of three: 3, 6, 9. But the last row only had two puppies! What happened to the last puppy?

Counting Eyes

When Myrtle saw 20 noses poking out of the box, she knew there were 20 little white mice. Then she counted 40 eyes. Each mouse has two eyes, and 20 twos makes 40.

You can check this by counting  by twos 20 times: 2, 4, 6, 8, 10, 12, 14, 16, 18, 20, 22, 24, 26, 28, 30, 32, 34, 36, 38, 40.

You can also say, "20 times 2 equals 40." And you can write this as 20 x 2 = 40.

When Myrtle saw 10 furry tails, she knew there were 10 little kittens. How many eyes do 10 kittens have all together? Count by twos to find out how much 10 x 2 is.

When Myrtle saw 12 thumping tails, she knew there were 12 little puppies. How many eyes do 12 puppies have? Count by twos to find out how much 12 x 2 is.

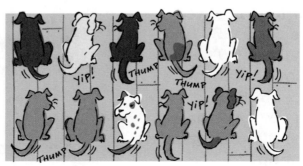

Pet Store Riddles

For each riddle, explain how you figured it out. You may want to draw pictures to help you solve them.

Riddle #1: There were four frogs in a store. How many legs did they have altogether?

Riddle #2: The ducks in a pet shop had 12 feet altogether. How many ducks were there?

Riddle #3: In the small fish tank, there were 12 fish. How many eyes did the fish have altogether?

Riddle #4: In the big fish tank, there were 50 eyes. How many fish were in there?

Riddle #5: A pet store had two geese and five turtles. How many feet and tails did they have altogether?

Riddle #6: A pet shop had six ducks and four frogs. How many feet and tails did they have altogether?

If your child is interested in riddles like these, make up others for him or her to solve. Experiment with different numbers. If you choose a number that's too difficult for your child, don't push, but instead choose numbers with which your child can be successful.

Turtle Patterns

A turtle has two eyes, four feet, one tail, and one shell. Two turtles have four eyes, eight feet, two tails, and two shells. How many eyes, feet, tails, and shells do three turtles have? Four? Five? More?

Make a chart. Look for patterns in the numbers of eyes, feet, and shells.

Turtle Patterns

Turtles	Eyes	Feet	Tails	Shells
1	2	4	1	1
2	4	8	2	2
3	6	12	3	3
4	?	?	?	?
5	?	?	?	?
6	?	?	?	?
?	?	?	?	?